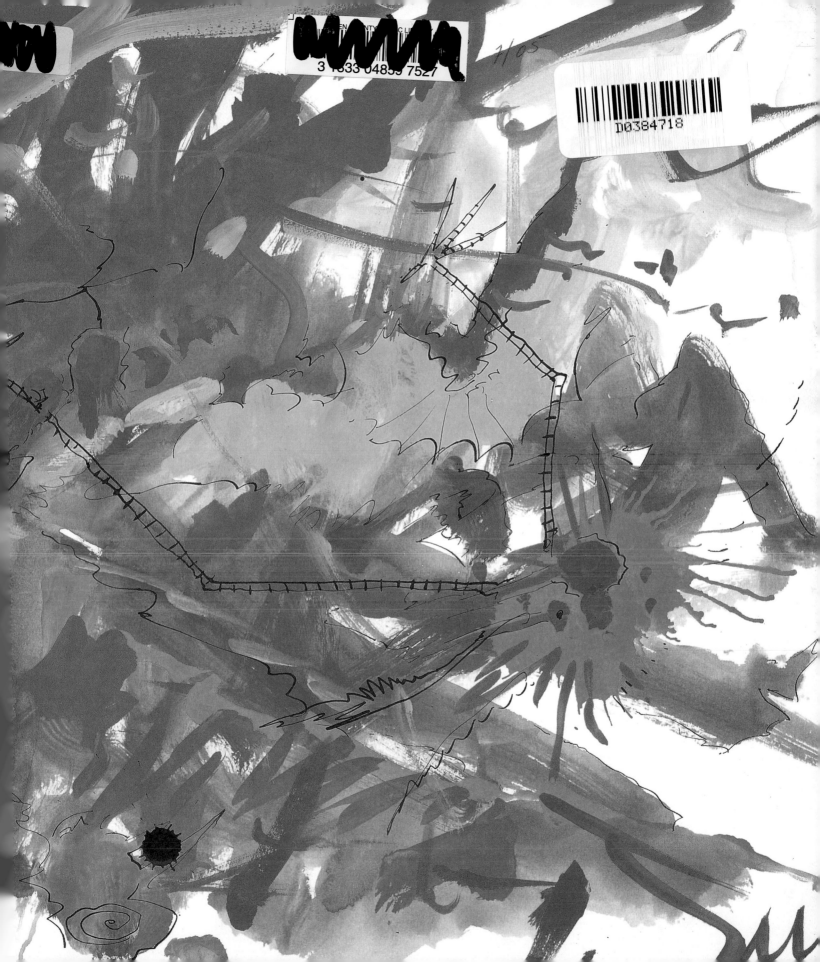

I Ain't Gonna Paint No More!

Karen Beaumont

ILLUSTRATED BY David Catrow

HARCOURT, INC.

Orlando   Austin   New York   San Diego   Toronto   London

Printed in Singapore

One day my mama caught me

paintin' pictures on the floor

and the ceiling

and the walls

and the curtains

and the door,

and I heard my mama holler

like I never did before...

"YA AIN'T A-GONNA PAINT NO MORE!"

3

I ain't gonna paint no more, no more,
I ain't gonna paint no more.

That's what I say...
but there ain't no way
that I ain't gonna paint no more.

So I take some red
and I paint my...

HEAD!

Now I ain't gonna paint no more.

Aw, what the heck!
Gonna paint my...

NECK!

Now I ain't gonna paint no more.

Still, I just can't rest
till I paint my...

CHEST!

Now I ain't gonna paint no more.

Guess there ain't no harm
if I paint my...

ARM!

Now I ain't gonna paint no more.

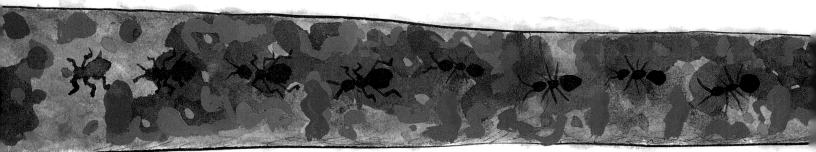

I ain't gonna paint no more, no more,
I ain't gonna paint no more.

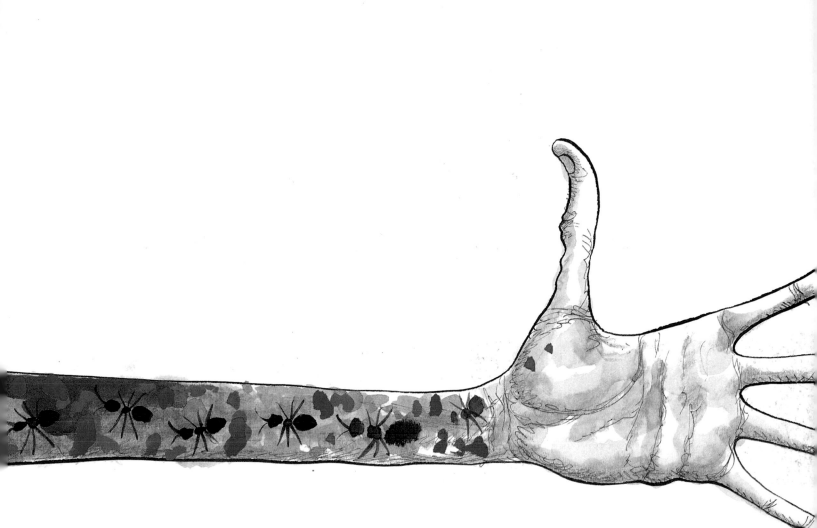

But I just can't stand
not to paint my…

HAND!

Now I ain't gonna paint no more.

Then I see some black
so I paint my...

BACK!

Now I ain't gonna paint no more.

Like an Easter egg,
gonna paint my…

LEG!

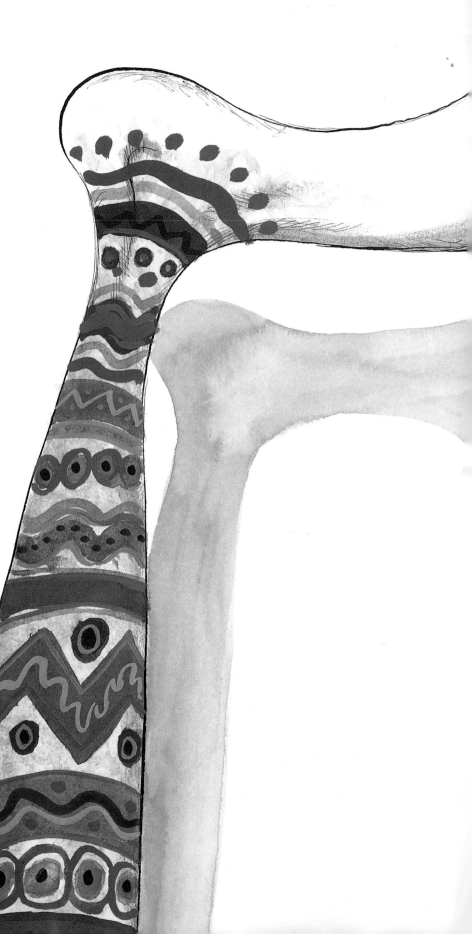

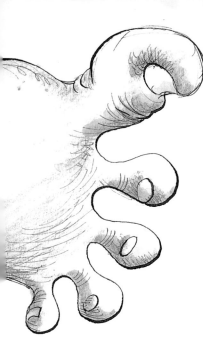

Now I ain't gonna paint no more.

Still, I ain't complete
till I paint my...

FEET!

Now I ain't gonna paint no more.

I ain't gonna paint no more, no more,
I ain't gonna paint no more.

But I'm such a nut,
gonna paint my—

Y'all don't faint...
'cause there ain't no paint!

So I ain't gonna paint no more!

For my beautiful daughters, Nicolyn and Christina,
who color my world with love—K. B.

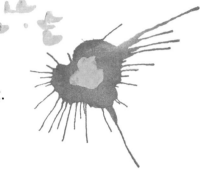

For Hillary, with love
Your greatest gifts are yet to be discovered—D. C.

Text copyright © 2005 by Karen Beaumont
Illustrations copyright © 2005 by David Catrow

www.HarcourtBooks.com

Library of Congress Cataloging-in-Publication Data
Beaumont, Karen.
I ain't gonna paint no more!/by Karen Beaumont; illustrated by David Catrow.
p.   cm.
Summary: In the rhythm of a familiar folk song, a child cannot resist adding one more dab of paint in surprising places.
[1. Painting—Fiction.   2. Stories in rhyme.]   I. Catrow, David, ill.   II. Title.
PZ8.3.B3845Ia   2005
[E]—dc22   2003027739
ISBN 0-15-202488-3

First edition

A C E G H F D B

The illustrations in this book were done in ink and paint.
The display lettering was created by Jane Dill.
The text type was set in Garamouche.
Color separations by Colourscan Co. Pte. Ltd., Singapore
Printed and bound by Tien Wah Press, Singapore
This book was printed on totally chlorine-free Stora Enso Matte paper.
Production supervision by Ginger Boyer
Designed by Judythe Sieck